ROYAL PAIN

SUDDENLY ROYAL

ROYAL PAIN

RAELYN DRAKE

MINNEAPOLIS

Darby Creek
A division of Lerner Publishing Group, Inc.
241 First Avenue North
Minneapolis, MN 55401 USA

For reading levels and more information, look up this title at www.lernerbooks.com.

Cover and interior images: Igor Klimov/Shutterstock.com (background texture); GoMixer/Shutterstock.com (coat of arms and lion); KazanovskyAndrey/iStock/Getty Images Plus (gold); mona redshinestudio/Shutterstock.com (crown).

Main body text set in Janson Text LT Std 12/17.5.
Typeface provided by Adobe Systems.

Library of Congress Cataloging-in-Publication Data

Names: Drake, Raelyn, author.
Title: Royal pain / Raelyn Drake.
Description: Minneapolis : Darby Creek, [2019] | Series: Suddenly royal | Summary:
   Seventeen-year-old Noah Fuller suddenly learns that he is heir to a dukedom in
   Evonia, but he must decide if he wants to follow in the family business or live his
   life as an ordinary citizen.
Identifiers: LCCN 2017048099 (print) | LCCN 2018007685 (ebook) |
   ISBN 9781541525979 (eb pdf) | ISBN 9781541525672 (lb : alk. paper) |
   ISBN 9781541526402 (pb : alk. paper)
Subjects: | CYAC: Identity—Fiction. | Nobility—Fiction.
Classification: LCC PZ7.1.D74 (ebook) | LCC PZ7.1.D74 Ro 2019 (print) | DDC
   [Fic]—dc23

LC record available at https://lccn.loc.gov/2017048099

Manufactured in the United States of America
1-44551-35482-2/15/2018

To Elizabeth Catherine, Molly Beth,
and Victoria Lynne

The Valmont Family of Evonia

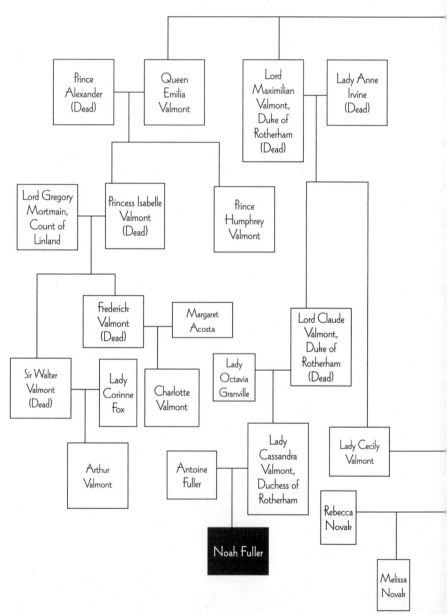

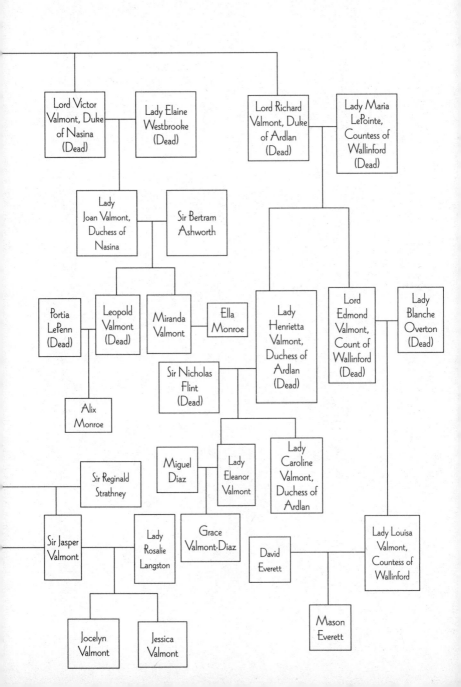

1

"We have to tell him."

Noah Fuller froze in the hallway when he heard his mom's hushed voice.

"We shouldn't, Cass—the timing just isn't right," Noah heard his dad say.

His parents were in the study with the door closed, speaking in low voices. Noah crept closer to listen as his mind raced through the possibilities of what his parents could be discussing.

"Antoine, this is going to change everything for him," his mom replied. "The sooner he knows, the better."

Noah felt his palms grow sweaty. *Oh no*, he thought, *are we moving?*

"Can't we wait until he's done with junior year? He's only got one more week before summer vacation. He has tests to study for."

Noah spared a guilty thought for the backpack full of homework and test-prep materials he left by the front door.

"We can't wait any longer. The funeral is next week."

Noah's breath snagged in his throat. He wrenched the study door open, not caring if his parents knew he had been eavesdropping. "What funeral?"

His parents jumped at his sudden entrance. His dad's mouth hung open a moment. His mom cleared her throat.

"Hi, honey, how was your—"

"Mom—"

"Your father and I were just talking—"

"Mom!" Noah repeated, louder. "Can you and Dad please just tell me what's going on?"

"Um . . ." His mom's voice faltered before she continued. "Grandfather Claude has passed away."

Noah's throat felt tight. He sank into the desk chair, half sad and half guilty he didn't feel any sadder about the death of his grandfather.

He hadn't been that close to his mom's side of the family. They lived in the tiny European country of Evonia, so he had never met them in person. His grandparents called twice a year: on his birthday and during the holidays. His Grandmother Octavia was nice enough but overly formal. Their conversations usually didn't make it past standard small-talk questions about school. But his Grandfather Claude had been warmer, more interested in what was going on in Noah's life beyond grades and college plans. He had been the one who first encouraged Noah's interest in archaeology.

And now he's gone. "I'm so sorry, Mom. Are you going to be okay?"

His mom managed a weak smile. "I'll survive." She exchanged a look with her husband, who sighed and gave a defeated shrug.

"Go ahead and tell him, Cass. You're right. He needs to know."

"There's *more*?" Noah asked, frowning. He couldn't imagine what sort of news could possibly be as important as his grandfather's death. "Hold on, are we flying out for the funeral?"

"That's part of what we need to tell you," his dad said.

"You always knew your grandpa as Grandfather Claude, but that's not all he was," his mom explained. "His full name was Lord Claude Valmont, Duke of Rotherham."

Is this some sort of elaborate prank? Noah thought. But his parents didn't really go for the whole practical joke thing. "He was a *duke*?" Noah shook his head, puzzled. "Like, an *actual* duke?"

His mom smiled again. "Yes. In fact, he was a member of the royal family of Evonia."

Noah thought back to the maps he had seen of the tiny country squished between France and Germany. He racked his brain for any more information about Evonia. "They have a queen, don't they?" Noah asked.

His mom nodded. "Their current ruler,

Queen Emilia, is my great-aunt."

Noah couldn't quite process this, so he backtracked to the part he could grasp. "So . . . we're flying to Evonia for the funeral. How long are we staying? A few days?"

"Umm. Actually, we're staying a little longer. It's a bit complicated," his mom explained. "You see, I didn't have any siblings. I was the *only* child of the Duke of Rotherham."

The realization of what his mom was hinting at hit Noah all at once. "So that means—?"

"Now that my father's gone, I've inherited the royal title. So I am now Lady Cassandra Valmont . . . Duchess of Rotherham."

"Of course you are," Noah said sarcastically. He scrunched his eyes shut for a moment. When he opened them, his parents were staring at him with worried expressions. "Why wouldn't you tell me this, like, *years* ago? How has it not come up *once* in seventeen years that I'm descended from a royal family?"

This time it was his dad who interjected. "I told you that your mom and I met while we were studying abroad. I just left out a few details. Like the fact that I met her while I was taking a tour of Rotherham Hall."

"I grew up there," Noah's mom explained, "and sometimes when I was bored I would lead tourist groups around and make up facts about Evonian history."

His dad pretended to be outraged. "You never told me you made those facts up!"

Noah's mom chuckled. "I fell in love with the cute American boy. We got married a year later, and we stayed in Evonia for a while. But when you were born we decided that you deserved a normal childhood."

"We moved to the States so you could grow up closer to my side of the family," his dad said, "like Grandpa and Grandma Fuller, and your aunt and cousins."

"Yeah, sure, I've had a great childhood," Noah said impatiently, "but I still feel like this was important information that you could've shared with me."

"We didn't want you to get caught up in that world," his mom said. "All the drama and expectations and high-society nonsense."

"You don't sound too excited about being a duchess, Mom," Noah said.

His mom grimaced. "It's just not the life I would have chosen for myself. But now that the title has passed to me, I don't really have a choice. My family needs me, and that's more important to me than my personal preferences." She smiled. "And besides, Evonia is a wonderful country."

"Are we moving to Evonia permanently?" Noah asked. He couldn't even imagine moving to a new town or state, and now he had to deal with the possibility of moving to a different country.

"We're not sure yet," his mom replied. "Our plan was to fly out for the funeral, and after that, I have some official business regarding the inheritance. So your dad and I will be staying in Evonia for the rest of the summer."

"The whole summer?" Noah said. It wasn't as bad as moving there forever, but he had been looking forward to spending summer break hanging out with his friends. Not being alone in a foreign country.

"You don't have to stay the whole summer if you don't want to," his dad said. "We'll buy you a plane ticket home whenever you've had enough. But we thought it was only fair that you get a look at the country, since it could be a big part of your future."

"What do you mean?" Noah asked.

"Well," his mom said, "the title is hereditary. So eventually when I die—which I hope won't be for a while, of course—the title will pass to you. You'll become Lord Noah Valmont, Duke of Rotherham."

"What if I don't want to be a duke?" Noah asked. He hadn't given that much thought to what he wanted to do after high school. But becoming royalty hadn't been anywhere on his list.

Noah's mom sighed. "I wouldn't blame you. I'm honestly not that thrilled either, but I feel I owe it to my father to keep his legacy going. And besides, my mother would never forgive me if I backed out." She smirked at Noah. "But I won't subject you to that kind of pressure and guilt. It's entirely up to you."

"Luckily," his dad said, "it's a decision you won't have to make for a long time. But you should still give Evonia a shot. It is honestly my favorite country in Europe."

Noah's mom added, "Plus, Noah, you'll be doing a huge favor for your grandmother. She's always wished she could have been closer to you. And now that she's a widow, I know she'll really appreciate having us all around to keep her company in that big old house."

Noah sighed. "Fine. I'm sure it will be great to see Grandmother Octavia, but I'm not making any other promises." He stood up. "I'm going to go take a walk, try to sort through all this."

"That's perfectly fine," his dad said.

Noah left the room, head buzzing.

2

A few days later, Noah was staring out
the window of a rental car as the Evonian
countryside flashed past. He had explained to
his friends that his grandfather had died and
he wouldn't be around town that summer,
but he couldn't bring himself to go further
into all of the details. He'd left out the part
about discovering that he was descended from
royalty, and that his mom had recently become
a duchess. Which left him with no one to talk
to about this whole weird situation, apart from
his parents.

His mom was driving the rental car with
the sunroof open. His dad was in the front
passenger seat, reading out loud from the

Evonian travel guide he had picked up at the airport.

"Look over there," his dad said, pointing at the crumbling remains of a stone building in the farm field they were about to pass. "It says here that it used to be a fortress, built by the ancient Evonians."

Noah perked up. "Ancient Evonians? We never learned about them in school." The ruins of the ancient fortress were covered in moss, but the walls still stood tall in many places, and Noah could easily see the outline of the old building. Back home, the oldest things in the fields tended to be barns with peeling paint, or rusted-out farm equipment. In Evonia, there were structures that were thousands of years old.

"The ancient Evonians were around at the same time as the ancient Romans in Great Britain," his mom explained. "I'm always surprised they don't appear in more history books. They didn't have a big empire like Rome or Greece or Egypt, but they were quite advanced, both with their culture and their technology."

"Wow, are you giving a book report, Mom?" Noah asked jokingly.

His mom laughed. "I know a lot more about this country's past than most people because my father taught me. He especially loved everything to do with history and archaeology."

"Grandfather Claude and I used to talk about archaeology sometimes," Noah said. "But he never mentioned anything about the ancient Evonians."

"That's because your mom and I made your grandparents promise they wouldn't tell you about the whole royalty thing until we thought you were ready," his dad said. "And a grandfather telling you he was sponsoring royal archaeological surveys may have given something away."

"Hey," Noah's mom said brightly to him. "Your grandfather had a small, private museum of ancient Evonian artifacts on the grounds of Rotherham Hall. I bet you'll have a lot of fun exploring that this summer."

***

The funeral was held at Rotherham Cathedral, an impressively large church a few miles away from Noah's grandparents' home. Once they arrived for the ceremony, Noah and his parents joined the line of mourners filing into the church. It was a small, private service for friends and family only, but the church foyer was crowded. Several volunteers were handing out paper programs and candles for the service.

A girl Noah's age handed him a long, thin candle. It had a paper cone around the base to catch any dripping wax.

"During the service," the girl explained, "Lady Octavia will light her own candle, and then the flame will be passed from person to person until all of the candles are lit."

"Thanks," Noah mumbled, looking at the program. It was printed on heavy, ivory-colored paper and embossed with silver cursive letters.

"I don't remember seeing you before," the girl said.

"Yeah, I'm kinda new here," Noah said. The girl was incredibly attractive, he realized, and he immediately felt self-conscious and guilty for thinking it. He had never been much of a ladies' man, and his grandfather's funeral certainly wasn't the time to practice his flirting. "I'm Noah Fuller," he said.

"Victoria Fontaine. But you can call me Tori," the girl said. "How did you know the duke?"

"Um, he was my grandfather actually."

Tori's eyes widened. "Oh! Wait, so that means your mother is Lady Cassandra Valmont?"

That caught Noah off guard. What had been news to him a week ago was apparently common knowledge for people in Evonia. "Uh, yeah, I guess she is."

He looked to where his parents stood in the line behind him. His mom was caught up in conversation with one of the volunteers, who addressed her as "Your Grace."

Noah shook his head and asked Tori, "How did you know my grandfather?"

Tori gave him a small smile and opened her mouth to respond, but at that moment

Noah's dad started pushing him along toward their seats. "Maybe I'll see you around?" was all she managed to get out.

3

The morning after the funeral, the rental car crunched along the gravel road through the woods that surrounded Rotherham Hall. Noah and his parents had spent the night at a small bed-and-breakfast near the cathedral to give his grandmother some privacy before they came to visit.

One more turn, and then the road emerged from the trees and cut across the smooth green lawn toward the house. Noah openly gaped. It was a huge stone building with double doors flanked by columns. He began to count the number of windows but almost immediately gave up.

"*This* is where you grew up?" Noah asked

his mom, completely shocked.

She grinned. "Home sweet home."

"If you think this is impressive," his dad said, "you should see the Valmont family's royal palace in the capital city, Alaborn. One time before your mom and I moved to the States, we stayed at the palace for a wedding. When I got up to use the bathroom in the middle of the night, I got lost for forty-five minutes."

Noah's mom snorted. "You did not!"

"Did too!" his dad said as they pulled up in front of the house. "After that I seriously considered leaving a trail of breadcrumbs whenever I ventured off alone." Noah's mom laughed.

Noah rolled his eyes and went to grab his suitcase out of the trunk of the car.

A man wearing a suit appeared at his side. "Allow me, my lord," he said, taking Noah's suitcase. "I will bring this up to your rooms."

"Uh, thanks," Noah said. "Did you just call me 'my lord'?"

"Yes, my lord," the man said. "You're the son of Lady Cassandra, after all."

"Ah, I see," Noah said, digging into the gravel drive with the toe of his shoe. "It's just, uh—I feel like that's going to be hard to get used to."

"Your Lordship is from America. Would 'sir' be a more comfortable form of address?"

"I'd prefer if you'd just call me Noah."

The man raised an eyebrow. "Between you and me, sir, your grandmother would never allow it. I will tell the others to use 'sir' when addressing Your Lordship."

And with that, the man whisked Noah's suitcase off toward the house.

"You know, Mom," Noah said as they walked up to the imposing front doors, "I don't think it's fair how much you nag me to clean my room when you grew up in a mansion with *servants*."

"Technically they're live-in staff. But I never said there weren't perks to being royalty," his mom said, smirking at him.

The doors swung open to let them in.

The entryway in Noah's house in America was small but cozy, filled with a shoe rack, coat hooks, and a basket for sorting the mail. The entryway at Rotherham Hall was two stories tall, with stained glass windows and a curving grand staircase.

Another man, whom Noah figured was the butler, approached Noah's mom. "Lady Octavia Granville is expecting you, Your Grace."

Of course she is, thought Noah. But maybe the butler had to follow a script for everyone who came to Rotherham Hall.

They followed him into the library, where Noah saw his grandmother sitting in a chair next to a large fireplace.

"Hi, Grandmother," Noah said, giving her a little wave. He suddenly wondered whether he was supposed to bow.

His grandmother broke into a wide smile when she saw them, which put Noah at ease. It was a smile he recognized—the exact same as his mom's smile.

"Cassandra, darling! And Antoine and Noah!" She rose to greet them.

Noah had never met his grandmother in person, and he wasn't sure if she was the hugging type or not. Luckily, he didn't have to guess. She took his hands in hers, leaned forward, and gave him a peck on each cheek.

His grandmother motioned for them to sit down on the other chairs around the fireplace. Noah noticed that she sat with her back stick straight, her legs crossed at the ankle and tucked under her chair. Even stranger, though, was the fact that Noah saw his mom sit like that as well. Usually his mom was the first one to snag the recliner at home. It was like she had flipped some switch from Cass Fuller posture to Lady Cassandra Valmont posture.

Noah's grandmother smoothed the skirt on her simple black dress. "It's so wonderful to see all of you. And especially you, Noah. You've grown into quite the handsome young man."

Noah felt his face flush. "Yeah, it's been great to finally see Evonia and start to learn about the family."

His grandmother raised an eyebrow. "Ah, yes, I forgot that you've only just learned about your royal heritage. And not a moment too soon. You enjoyed your 'normal' childhood in America, I trust?"

Noah's mom cleared her throat. "He certainly did, Mother."

"And what do you think of our beloved country?" Noah's grandmother asked him.

"It's great," Noah said. "All the ancient Evonian stuff is really cool."

His grandmother smiled wistfully. "One of your grandfather's great joys in life was his study of the ancient Evonian culture. It makes my heart glad to see you following in Claude's footsteps. I'm sure your mother has told you about the museum on the grounds?"

Noah nodded. "I can't wait to see it."

"You're in luck, then, because I have something special planned for the museum. Right now, it is a private collection, but your grandfather always felt that the people of Evonia should have more opportunities to learn about their past. It was always his dream to make the museum a public institution."

"Isn't the museum in your backyard?" Noah asked.

His grandmother chuckled. "The 'backyard' of Rotherham Hall is quite extensive. Visitors will be able to come and go without disturbing my peace. And it's what Claude would have wanted. At the end of July I will host a garden party to celebrate the grand opening of the Rotherham Museum of Ancient Evonian Artifacts. The party will be a fundraiser, and all donations will go toward educational programs and resources for the students of Evonia, so that they may learn more about the history of our proud nation."

"That's very admirable," Noah's dad said.

"If you are willing, Noah," his grandmother said, "I would love to have your help in getting the museum ready to open. I'm afraid it is in rather rough shape right now. There will be some cleaning, yes, but I'll also need help arranging the artifacts, creating the signs for the displays using the information in your grandfather's old notes, and so on."

"That sounds like an amazing opportunity," Noah said. "But July is getting pretty late into the summer. I mean, I guess I could stay that long if you really need me, but I was hoping to . . ." Seeing the look on his grandmother's face, Noah stopped short of saying that he was hoping to go home sooner than that.

Noah's grandmother pursed her lips and shot a look at her daughter. "It was my understanding that you were all going to stay for the entire summer."

"Antoine and I will be here," Noah's mom said. "But we agreed that Noah could decide when he wanted to leave."

"I would have thought," Noah's grandmother said, "that Noah would want to spend as much time as possible in Evonia. After all, he will one day be the Duke of Rotherham himself—"

"I'm still not sold on the whole duke thing, actually . . ." Noah stopped short again when he saw his grandmother's expression. It was a lot easier to say that when he wasn't being stared down by a seventy-year-old royal.

His grandmother pressed her mouth into a thin line. "The Rotherham title is not a thing that can be cast aside on a whim. You are the only heir after your mother."

Noah almost wished his grandmother would shout at him. Her cold primness was somehow worse than an angry outburst.

"Uh," he stammered. "I'm not ready to commit to anything just yet."

"Yes, Mother," Noah's mom added more firmly. "We're letting him decide."

The thin line of his grandmother's mouth was growing even thinner.

Behind him, Noah heard the library doors at the far end of the room swing open.

His grandmother smiled suddenly. "I'm sure we will find *something* to make that decision easier for you."

Before Noah had time to wonder about his grandmother's sudden change of mood and the scheming glint in her eye, she rose and gestured to the people who had just entered the library.

"May I introduce Lady Annabeth Sharpe, Baroness of Colwin. No relation to the Valmonts, but the Sharpes are an old and prestigious Evonian family. And this is Victoria Fontaine."

Noah jumped to his feet and turned around.

"Tori?" he said, recognizing her from the funeral.

"Hi, Noah!" Tori said, eyes sparkling. "I figured I might run into you again."

"Annabeth and Victoria are going to be our guests at Rotherham Hall this summer," Noah's grandmother said. "I assumed Noah would enjoy having the company of people his own age."

"That will be great," Noah's mom exclaimed. "Antoine and I aren't going to be around much." And with a surprised look from Noah, added, "We'll have to spend a lot of our time at the family's legal offices in Alaborn to deal with all the paperwork of inheriting the royal title."

"It's a pleasure to meet you, Lord Noah," Annabeth said, extending her hand. Noah took it, feeling a little awkward, but since she didn't seem to be expecting a handshake, he let go again.

"Likewise," he said. "And please just call me Noah—no one else will."

Annabeth giggled. "Oh good! All the formal titles—Lady Annabeth, or Baroness, or Your Ladyship—they always sound so stuffy! My friends just call me Beth."

"And no one ever calls me Victoria," Tori chimed in.

"I don't see why not," Noah's grandmother sniffed. "Victoria is a perfectly lovely name."

Tori smiled sweetly. "Of course it is. But it is also my mother's name. So it saves everyone a lot of confusion if I go by Tori."

"Will your parents be staying here as well?" Noah's mom asked.

Tori shook her head. "They're spending the summer traveling."

"Mine too," Beth said. "Which is why we're very grateful that Lady Octavia has invited us to spend the summer at Rotherham Hall. Otherwise I would've been so bored and lonely! I'm excited to check out all the hiking trails."

"And I can't wait to see the museum again!" Tori said. "My parents were helping Lord

Claude with the renovation," she explained
to Noah.

"Oh yeah, the museum," Beth sighed.
But then her tone changed as she added "We
agreed we would help get it ready for the
wonderful garden party."

It wasn't lost on Noah that Beth sounded
more enthusiastic about the party than
the museum.

Noah's grandmother clapped her hands
together lightly. "I'm sure Noah and his
parents would like a chance to see their
rooms and take a couple of hours to relax
and refresh. I've arranged for luncheon to be
served at one o'clock in the main dining room."

4

Noah was grateful for the chance to have
a moment to himself. He was beginning
to feel the effects of jet lag. He took a nap,
then showered and looked through his
clothes for something to wear to lunch, or
"luncheon," as his grandmother had called
it. He wondered what the dress code was for
a luncheon.

He dumped the contents of his suitcase on
the bed and sighed. He had brought one suit
for the funeral, but that seemed too formal
for a private meal. On the other hand, since
he hadn't been planning on staying more than
a couple of weeks, the rest of his clothes were
all casual. After debating for a minute, Noah

put on his funeral suit again, trying his best to smooth out the rumpled fabric.

There was a knock at his bedroom door.

"Come in!" he called, focused on trying to knot his tie.

"Your grandmother is *not* going to be happy if you try to wear that to lunch," his mom said as she popped her head into his bedroom.

Noah stared at the reflection of his lopsided tie knot and frowned. "I don't really have any other options," he muttered, pulling out the knot to start over again.

"Have you checked the closet yet?" his mom asked.

Noah paused. "No, why?"

"Your fairy godmother wanted to make sure you had something nice to wear to the ball." His mom grinned. "By which I mean your grandmother asked me for your measurements and bought you an entire wardrobe to get you through the summer."

Sure enough, the closet was full of clothes. Slacks, button ups, sports coats, and at least fifteen different suits in varying colors and styles. All of which looked nicer than anything Noah had ever owned.

"Wow," he whispered.

His mom smiled. "Why don't you change? You're probably going to want one of the less formal suits. Open collar, no tie. Perfect for a summer luncheon." She turned to leave. "Oh, and your grandmother also insisted on buying you all the accessories you could ever need: cufflinks, ties, bowties, watches, even sunglasses." His mother gestured to the drawers on either side of his closet.

Not long after, Noah walked briskly toward the dining room. He had gotten distracted trying to decide which of his suits would be considered less formal, and now he was running late. His grandmother did not seem like the sort of person who tolerated lateness.

Noah burst into the dining room at one minute past one, according to his new watch.

His grandmother smiled at him from her place at the head of the dining table. "How nice of you to join us, Noah. We were about to send out a search party."

His parents, Beth, and Tori were already seated. The dining table was long, and there were a few different open chairs. Catching his breath, Noah ignored his grandmother's comment about his tardiness, and went to sit in the open spot by Tori.

"Noah, darling," his grandmother called. "I think you'll find that the place settings are labeled with name cards. You are supposed to sit next to Annabeth." Noah's grandmother stared intently at Beth.

Noah paused, halfway into his chair, and looked across the table to Beth, who flipped around the place card with his name on it. She shrugged and smiled sheepishly.

Noah cleared his throat. He walked down one side of the incredibly long table and back up the other in awkward silence. Beth beamed at him as he took his place next to her. He snuck a glance at Tori on the other side of the table. Tori suppressed a smirk and darted her eyes to the side like she wanted to roll her eyes but didn't dare.

Noah thought it was a bit odd that his

grandmother had set out place cards for a small family lunch. But, he decided, it was probably just one of those silly rules of royalty. He would have rather sat by Tori and talked with her about his grandfather, but Beth seemed nice enough.

One wall of the dining room was lined with glass French doors that opened out onto a paved terrace overlooking the grounds behind the house. Noah could see why his grandmother had laughed when he used the word "backyard." Beyond the terrace railing, the perfectly cut lawn seemed to go on forever under the pale blue sky. Near the forest that surrounded the grounds, he could see a line of tall hedges and a brick building about a third of the size of Rotherham Hall.

"That's your grandfather's museum," his grandmother said, as if reading Noah's thoughts. "It's a little on the small side, but I think we'll manage. It used to be a guest cottage."

Noah raised his eyebrows but didn't say what he was thinking—that the guest cottage was bigger than his house.

Octavia rang a delicate silver bell, then placed it back down on the table next to her crystal water goblet.

At her signal, a number of servants entered the room carrying bowls of soup, which they placed in front of the diners. Noah turned to say thank you like he would to a waiter at a restaurant, but the servants had already glided back out of the dining room.

Noah stared at his soup, and felt slightly puzzled. The bowl was cold, and the contents looked more like salsa than soup. He wanted to ask what sort of dish it was, but he seemed to be the only one who wasn't familiar with it—even his non-royal father looked at ease—and he didn't want to embarrass himself.

Beth nudged him slyly with her elbow. "It's gazpacho," she whispered out of the corner of her mouth. "A cold vegetable soup."

"Oh, of course, I knew that. I'd recognize it anywhere," Noah said in a sarcastic whisper back.

Beth suppressed a giggle and Noah gave her a grateful smile.

The gazpacho not only looked like salsa, it tasted like it. But once he got over how different it was, Noah found that he didn't mind gazpacho.

The soup course was followed by two more courses, each one more elaborate than the last. Noah was worried about all the rules of proper eating, but not enough to ruin his appetite. Everything tasted delicious. Still, he was thankful that Beth subtly pointed out which fork to use for each course. It made things considerably easier without drawing attention to his lack of experience with fine dining.

When the servants returned a fourth time carrying covered silver dishes Noah groaned jokingly. "I'm stuffed," he whispered to Beth. When the dessert course turned out to be strawberry shortcake with freshly whipped cream, he added, "But somehow I think I'll manage to carry on."

Beth laughed. "A four-course luncheon is nothing. To be honest, I'm surprised your grandmother left out the salad course."

"If a lunch can have five courses, I shudder to think of what dinner involves." Noah took a bite of his dessert. "Although, if all the courses are this good, you won't hear any complaints from me. I never eat like this back home."

"I've always wanted to visit America, you know, but my parents always insist on vacationing in France," Beth said. "So tell me—what's it like living in America?" Tori looked up at him too, clearly interested in what Noah had to say.

The question caught him off guard. Noah had never really thought about the United States as being any different than other places. "Uh, just like the movies, I guess. Only with fewer spontaneous dance numbers and flashy race cars. I'm much more interested in hearing what life in Evonia is like. I still don't know that much about the country, really."

"It's absolutely lovely here," Beth said. "In my opinion, this country is—"

"It's just like the movies," Tori cut in. "Only with fewer submarines and a lot less yodeling."

Noah snorted, then tried to turn it into a cough when his grandmother shot him a disapproving look from the head of the table.

"She's joking of course," Beth explained.

"What a shame," Noah said. "I really only came to Evonia for the yodeling."

It was Tori's turn to try to hide her laughter. Beth's laugh sounded a little forced, as though she wasn't quite sure she got the joke.

"I hope that our natural Evonian charm and good looks can make up for our lack of yodeling," Tori said, staring at him over the rim of her glass.

Noah smiled at her. "I think they will," he said. Then he realized he was holding Tori's eye a little too long and went back to his dessert.

5

After a solid twelve hours of sleep, Noah was
starting to feel refreshed after the stress of
all that had happened the past week. He was
prepared to lie in bed for another hour or two
when he realized that his grandmother might
have certain expectations of when he should
be up in the morning. He stood in front of
his closet, stretching sleepily and trying to
figure out what he should wear. The suit he
had worn the day before had been so expensive
looking that he had felt self-conscious wearing
it. He planned to spend the day exploring the
grounds, and he wanted an outfit that he didn't
have to worry about getting dirty. He looked
through all of the clothes his grandmother had

bought him, before coming to the conclusion that royalty didn't think of casual clothes in the same way he did. Feeling slightly reckless, he picked an outfit from his suitcase. But he couldn't resist grabbing a pair of sunglasses from the drawer before he went downstairs.

He found his parents out on the patio that opened up off the dining room. Luckily, his grandmother didn't seem to be anywhere in sight, so he didn't have to face her disapproval of his outfit choice just yet.

His mom was reading the newspaper, while his dad browsed on his tablet.

"Good morning, sleepyhead," Noah's mom said brightly.

"This is early for you," his dad said, checking the time. "We never see you up this early back home."

Noah shrugged and plopped down on the chair next to them. "I think my sleep schedule is still out of whack from the time difference."

After a little while Noah noticed that the newspaper his mom was reading wasn't in English. He tilted his head to get a better look at the words. "I didn't know you spoke French, Mom."

"I'm a bit rusty, I'm afraid," his mom said. "But French and German are two of the official languages of Evonia besides English, so I need to brush up on my skills."

"Why did you guys let me take so many years of Spanish classes, then?" Noah asked.

"Because Spanish is a very useful language," his dad said. "Just not in Evonia."

"So it won't do me any good anymore, I guess." Noah sighed.

"Of course it will! Don't worry," his dad added, "your mom and I aren't going to move here full-time until after you've finished high school. And while you're in college, you can decide whether to spend your summers in America or in Evonia."

"This whole thing is so weird. It feels so wrong," Noah grumbled, looking out over the Rotherham Hall grounds.

"Don't worry, you'll get used to it eventually. And even if you don't," Noah's mom added in a stage whisper, "that's okay too.

I, for one, will never blame you if you decide this isn't your scene."

"Your grandmother will definitely mind, though," his dad said, grinning mischievously.

His mom snorted. "Oh yeah, I mean *she* would probably be furious, but *we* promise to support whatever decision you make, one hundred percent."

Noah laughed. "Thanks, guys, I appreciate it." *More than you know*, he added to himself. "So, what's the schedule for today?"

"Your mom and I are taking the train to Alaborn on official business," Noah's dad said. "We're leaving in a few hours, and we'll be back in three or four days."

"What am I supposed to do in the meantime? *Please* don't leave me here alone with Grandmother," Noah said, only half-joking. As soon as the words left his mouth, he whipped around, suddenly paranoid that he would find his grandmother standing right behind him. But the coast was clear.

"You have Beth and Tori to hang out with," his dad pointed out.

"Yes," his mom chimed in, "they seem like really nice girls."

His mom and dad were using the same tone of voice they used whenever they met a female friend of Noah's who they thought might have girlfriend potential. Noah rolled his eyes.

"Yeah, they're both great," Noah said, "but I'm not really looking for an Evonian girlfriend when I'm not going to be here that long anyway."

His mom raised an eyebrow. "I think your grandmother might have other plans," she muttered.

"What do you mean?" Noah asked.

His mom looked like she was about to explain when her expression suddenly froze. Looking over Noah's shoulder she called out, "Good morning, Mother!"

Noah turned to see his grandmother beaming at them all.

"And what a lovely morning it is," she said. "I was just telling Annabeth here that it would be the perfect time to go explore Claude's museum."

Noah gave Beth a friendly nod. She had followed his grandmother out onto the patio. He was glad to see that she had opted for shorts and a t-shirt as well, although she managed to pull it off a little more fashionably.

"I'm ready when you are, Noah," Beth said brightly.

"You don't need to worry about breakfast," Noah's grandmother said. "I've already arranged for one of the staff to drop off a picnic basket at the museum, so you can eat there."

"Aren't we going to wait for Tori?" Noah asked, looking around for her.

"I'm sure she'll be along shortly," his grandmother said, making small shooing motions with her hands. "You and Annabeth can start walking over, and Tori can catch up whenever she's ready."

Noah thought his grandmother seemed in an awful hurry for them to leave. "It seems like it'd be easier to all walk over together," he said.

Noah thought he saw his grandmother shoot Beth a knowing look.

"Tori won't mind," Beth said, with a smile a bit wider than seemed appropriate. "Come on, let's go, Noah."

Noah was about to follow when he heard Tori's voice behind him.

"Sorry, sorry!" Tori called, dashing up to join them. "I didn't realize we were on such a tight schedule today."

"That's fine, I don't mind waiting," Noah said, looking back at his grandmother, a gesture that his grandmother pretended to ignore. "Shall we?"

The three of them set off across the lawn for the museum across the lush green grass and past a hedge maze. Fifteen minutes later, Noah was beginning to understand why the few gardeners they had passed on the way had been driving golf carts rather than walking themselves. He was just starting to appreciate how large the Rotherham Hall grounds truly were. He was definitely tired and a little bit hot by the time they reached the museum.

For something called a "guest cottage," the building was just as oversized in person as it had looked from a distance. It was made of red brick, its windows framed by flowering vines. A large, checkered blanket had already been set out for them on the front steps along with an overflowing picnic basket. The person who had delivered it was nowhere to be seen, and Noah was reminded of the Easter Bunny as he helped himself to a hard-boiled egg.

The three of them ate their breakfast on the front steps in the morning sunshine. The basket was filled with enough food to feed an army. *It turns out even picnics have multiple courses when royals are involved*, Noah thought to himself. The meal was so over the top that he was torn between amusement and exasperation. When they had finished eating and packed the leftovers back into the basket, Noah and the girls headed up the steps into the museum. The building was cool and dimly lit. Furniture covered with dusty drop cloths filled most of the rooms. It was hard to see how it could be turned into a public space.

"This way," Tori said, pointing. "The parlor is the only room of the museum that's been finished so far. Lord Claude wanted to create an example of what the rest of the museum would look like when it was completed."

The parlor had been cleared of all furniture. It was a spacious room, with gleaming hardwood floors and a fresh coat of paint. Glass cases stood against the walls, labeled with plaques that listed the items inside and the history of each one.

Tori flicked one of the light switches near the door, and hidden LED lights inside the cases glowed, illuminating the artifacts. Here and there, Noah could even see the glint of gold and the flash of gemstones.

Noah sucked in his breath. "Whoa," he said.

Tori grinned. "I'm glad you like it. My parents helped Lord Claude design it."

"That's right. You said they were involved with my grandfather's museum." Noah suddenly remembered.

"My parents are archaeologists," Tori explained. "Lord Claude funded many of their digs, and so my parents donated a lot of their finds to his museum. Lord Claude was so fond of ancient Evonian artifacts. That's how he became friends with my parents in the first place."

Noah smiled to himself, recalling his discussions with his grandfather about ancient history and archaeology.

"This is only part of the collection," Tori explained. "Lady Octavia wants the whole place to look as good as this room by the time the museum opens at the end of July."

Beth bit her lip. "The whole place? With only the three of us?"

Tori shook her head. "No, Lady Octavia is hiring professionals to do all of the heavy lifting, floor polishing—stuff like that. But she wants us to be the ones in charge of getting the artifacts ready to display. You know, dusting, sorting, labeling. Someone from the archaeology department at Alaborn University will be supervising of course."

"Oh," Beth said, "that doesn't sound too bad. I'm always willing to help out, but I wouldn't want to have to spend *all* summer stuck inside this gloomy old place."

Noah realized Beth was looking at him as though she expected him to agree with her. He forced himself to return her smile, but deep down he knew that there was nothing he would rather do than spend his summer in his grandfather's museum.

"It says here that this small clay horse was most likely a child's toy," Tori said, reading from the label next to the case. "And apparently there's a thumbprint in the clay left by the person who made it." She leaned toward Noah, eyes flashing with excitement. "Can you imagine? A thumbprint belonging to a person who lived over four thousand years ago."

"Wow," Noah whispered, resisting the urge to push his nose up against the glass case to get a better look at the tiny clay animal. He could feel his heart beating quicker, but that had less to do with the artifact and more to do with Tori standing so close to him.

For the past week, Noah, Tori, and Beth

had been working on the museum. Today they'd spent all morning dusting the dining room and ballroom so that the painters could get started. Now they had returned to the finished parlor, taking a much-needed break by browsing the display cases. Noah was thrilled to have a chance to examine the artifacts more carefully. Tori seemed just as interested, but he had a feeling Beth was getting bored. She had been staring longingly out the window, her silence punctuated by occasional polite noises in response to Noah's comments.

"Ooh!" exclaimed Beth suddenly, pointing to something in the next case over and sounding more excited than she had all morning. "*This* is absolutely gorgeous."

Noah walked over to look. It was a crown, formed of gold leaves that overlapped to give the impression of a wreath. Flowers made of rubies seemed to sprout from the branches. It was certainly eye-catching, but Noah couldn't help thinking that the simple clay toy was cooler somehow. It had a lot more character than the overly perfect crown.

"The label says that this crown once belonged to Queen Helen herself," Beth said, sounding awestruck. "She was one of Evonia's first queens from ancient times," she explained to Noah.

"This museum—the collection—all of it is amazing," Noah said. "I can't wait for the grand opening."

"It will be hard work to get it ready in time," Tori said, "but it will be worth it. Do you want to go through some of the collection boxes they just brought up from the basement storage?"

Noah opened his mouth to respond with an enthusiastic yes when Beth cut in.

"It's already past noon," she said, "and we haven't had anything to eat since breakfast. Why don't we head back to the main house for a quick bite, then we can take horses out to ride the trail along the bluffs. It has the best view, possibly in all of Evonia. And," she added, "there used to be an ancient Evonian outpost along the bluffs, so there's bound to be some old ruins to explore."

"That sounds great, Beth," Tori said, "but I'm not very good on horseback."

"And I haven't been on a horse since a pony at camp tried to throw me off," Noah said. "Why don't we just hike instead?"

Beth bit her lip thoughtfully. "It's too far to walk . . ." Then her face brightened. "But I have an even better idea!"

***

Noah sped along the trail on his moped, enjoying the feeling of the wind whipping past him. Tori and Beth rode ahead of him on their own mopeds. When they had explained their afternoon plans to Noah's grandmother at lunch, she had tried to convince them that there were only two mopeds available in all of Rotherham Hall. But after Noah stoutly refused her suggestion that he share a moped with Beth, a staff member had conveniently discovered a third.

Noah rolled his eyes at the memory. It was painfully obvious that his grandmother was pushing Beth at him. He just couldn't

51

figure out why. Beth was nice enough, sure, but he felt like his grandmother had some deeper motive.

He pushed these thoughts aside, forcing himself to just enjoy the moment. It had rained off and on for the past week, but today the sun was shining brightly and the sky was a cloudless, vibrant blue. The trail was bordered by a low stone wall, and beyond that the bluffs dropped abruptly down toward the river. Beth had been right about the view. He looked out over the patchwork of golden fields and green pastures to the mountains in the distance. He could just make out the snowcapped peaks through the hazy summer air.

They rounded a corner, and Tori held up her hand, motioning them to stop. Noah pulled up alongside her and parked his moped. Just off the trail, he could see the remains of a stone building. In some places, the walls and stairs were still visible. In other places, time had worn the stone down into rubble.

Tori removed her helmet and shook out her hair.

Beth took off her fingerless leather gloves and laid them on the seat of her moped, placing her helmet neatly on top. She pushed her sunglasses up on top of her head and sighed contentedly. "Oh, fresh air and sunshine, it's been too long!" she said playfully.

"You make it sound like the museum is some sort of dungeon," Tori smirked. "But it *is* great to get outside for a while." She looked out over the valley. "Hey, look! You can see Rotherham Hall from here!"

Noah shaded his eyes. "It's so big, I bet you could see it from space."

"If you think Rotherham Hall is big," Beth said, "you should see the—"

"Royal palace in Alaborn?" Noah finished. He laughed. "Yeah, so I've been told."

Beth made her way into the ruins, scrambling over rocks and up half-buried flights of stairs. "Let's explore!" she called back, before disappearing behind a stone pillar.

Tori smiled at Noah and they followed Beth.

"Do you think we'll find any undiscovered ancient Evonian treasures?" Noah asked Tori.

Tori shook her head. "This outpost was one of the first ancient Evonian sites to be abandoned. I don't think there've been any artifacts left to find here since your grandfather was a child."

"Hey, you never know, right?" Noah ran a hand over the rough, mossy stone of a nearby wall. "Although, the ruins themselves are incredible enough," he said.

Tori smiled. "You sound just like Lord Claude. I've heard this was one of your grandfather's favorite places to come and be alone."

Noah enjoyed being compared to his grandfather. "I'm sure it's a great place to be alone," he said quietly, "but it's even better having someone to share it with."

Tori smiled. Their eyes met, and Noah's stomach did a somersault as she leaned her face closer to his.

"Hurry up, you slowpokes," Beth called from the top of a set of uneven stone steps. She laughed and turned. Then they heard her shriek and she vanished from sight.

"Beth!" Noah yelled. He and Tori raced up the steps to the spot where they had last seen their friend.

Beth was on the ground. "I think I twisted my ankle," she said, teeth gritted in pain.

Tori bent swiftly to examine the injured ankle. "Can you move your foot?" she asked.

Beth twitched her foot and let out a small yelp.

Tori turned to Noah. "We'll have to get her back to Rotherham Hall. Lady Octavia's family physician will be able to help. He makes house calls all the time."

Rotherham Hall has its own doctor? Noah thought. *Why am I not surprised?*

"How are we going to do that?" Beth asked. She whimpered as she pushed herself carefully into a seated position. "There's no way I can ride my moped with my ankle like this."

"One of us will have to ride double," Tori said. "Noah, why don't you ride ahead and tell Lady Octavia what happened? I'll bind Beth's ankle as best I can, and then we'll follow more slowly."

Beth looked from Tori to Noah. "But Lady Octavia would probably prefer . . ." Noah gave Beth a startled look, wondering why was she thinking of his grandmother at a time like this.

Beth must have noticed his expression because she quickly added "What if you ride ahead, Tori, and Noah could tend to my ankle. You're a better moped rider, so you'll get to back to Rotherham Hall much more quickly than Noah could."

Noah wanted to help, but saw a huge flaw in Beth's plan. He shook his head. "Sorry, Beth, I have no idea how to do first aid for a twisted ankle. Tori seems to know what she's doing."

Tori nodded. "Your ankle is already swelling," she explained. "I need to stabilize it so you don't do more damage to it before we ride back."

The sun was starting to edge toward the horizon, and Noah suddenly realized he wasn't sure he knew how to get back to Rotherham Hall from here. Being able to see the place didn't do him much good since the road to get there twisted and branched. "Wait, this is kind of a silly argument anyway," he pointed out. "I'll just call my grandmother. She can send someone with a truck that can fit us and our mopeds, and we can ride back in style."

"Great idea," Tori said. "The trail up here isn't big enough for cars, but they can pick us up at the base of the cliffs. That won't be too far if we have help getting Beth down."

"And that way we don't have to split up while we wait for help to arrive," Beth said brightly.

Tori set to work bandaging Beth's ankle using a first aid kit that had been tucked in the storage netting of her moped. Meanwhile, Noah called his grandmother and explained the situation.

"Why didn't you just take Annabeth on your moped and drive her back to the house?" his grandmother asked. "That would have been very dashing and chivalrous."

"*Grandmother!*" Noah hissed under his breath.

"You're right, though, I suppose it does make more sense to send a car to pick you up. It's a short drive to the bluffs. I'll have my butler fetch the doctor, and have a car of suitable size brought round from the garage. Stay where you are—the butler will bring crutches for Lady Annabeth."

Noah breathed a sigh of relief. "That sounds great, thank you so much, Grand—"

"Will the three of you be late to dinner, then?" his grandmother asked.

"What?" Noah asked. "Yes, of course we'll be late to dinner. I'm sure your butler can reheat a plate of leftovers for us once we're rescued. Goodbye, Grandmother," he said firmly, and hung up before she could express her outrage over concepts like "reheating" and "leftovers."

He turned back to Beth and Tori. "She's sending a rescue party. So now we just have to sit tight and wait until our knight in shining armor arrives."

Beth nodded her approval, but Tori was still busy wrapping Beth's ankle and didn't respond.

Noah kneeled down next to the two girls and picked up the roll of tape. When Tori needed more tape for the bandaging, he tore some off and handed it to her. He and Tori silently worked together wrapping Beth's ankle until Tori was satisfied with the job.

"There, how does that feel?" Tori asked Beth.

Beth gave Tori a weak but genuine smile. "It already feels much better. Thank you, Tori." Then thoughtfully she added, "You know, you two make a great team."

Noah blushed and looked away as he heard Tori mumble a thank you. After a short awkward pause Beth started up a new conversation. The three of them joked and chatted while they watched the peach-and-purple sunset blaze over the river valley.

Soon the car arrived on the road below the bluff. The butler brought up a pair of crutches for Beth and helped her stand up.

Tori packed up the first aid kit. But when Noah went to grab his backpack, Beth turned to him suddenly.

"I think I dropped my phone when I fell," she said. "Could you two stay behind and look for it?"

Noah opened his mouth to argue that he had just seen her stick her phone in her jeans pocket less than five minutes ago. But then Beth gave him an exaggerated wink, with a meaningful glance at Tori.

He felt his face flush with a mix of embarrassment and gratitude as he realized that Beth was trying to give him a chance to be alone with Tori. It must be obvious to Beth that he and Tori had a connection. But they never had any privacy at Rotherham Hall, with his grandmother hovering over them and making pointed remarks.

"Ah yeah, sure, no problem," he said, playing along and giving Beth a grateful smile.

"No rush," Beth called back as the butler guided her to the trail. "It will take me *forever* to hobble down to the car."

Noah and Tori looked at each other. This was the first time they had been alone and Noah wasn't quite sure what to do. He didn't want to say the wrong thing so he just stood there silently.

"Well, I guess we should get to it, then." Tori said after a minute.

"Get to what?" Noah asked.

"Umm, looking for Beth's phone," Tori answered, giving him a curious look.

"Oh yeah, that." Noah had been so distracted he had completely forgotten about the phone. *Get it together, Noah. Calm down*, Noah told himself. He followed Tori carefully down the stone steps where Beth had fallen and started scanning the ground alongside her, knowing that they wouldn't find anything.

"You know, this place reminds me of a book my dad used to read to me as a kid," Tori said absentmindedly. "It was about a kid that went on adventures hunting treasure. When I was really young, that's sort of what I thought my parents were doing on archaeological digs—going on adventures for treasure." She picked up a twig off the ground and looked up at him cautiously. "That probably sounds really stupid."

Noah smiled at Tori. "I don't think it sounds stupid at all. I've never been to a dig before, but that all makes sense. They are going on adventures and looking for buried treasure. It just might not be a shiny crown or gold."

Tori grinned back at him and continued with more confidence this time. "Yeah! It's actually super cool to be on a dig site. If we have time, maybe we could go see my parents at their current site . . ."

"I would absolutely love that!" Noah said.

The two locked eyes, both beaming. "Me too." said Tori.

The date of the museum's grand opening drew
closer. The days settled into a comfortable
routine as Noah found himself getting more
used to the way things were done at Rotherham
Hall. He would never have imagined he would
spend his summer dressing up for every meal,
but he was finally starting to get the hang of
which fork went with which course.

Noah's mom and dad spent most of their
time traveling to and from Alaborn and
other parts of Evonia, but when they were
at Rotherham Hall, Noah enjoyed spending
time with them. His mom was teaching
Noah how to ride a horse, and he and his dad
watched movies together. Sometimes Noah

and his parents spent hours just sitting on the patio, relaxing and talking. It was almost like a normal summer back home—until the butler appeared and addressed his mom as "Your Grace."

When his parents weren't around, Noah, Tori, and Beth spent most mornings getting the museum ready. Then in the afternoons they would go exploring. Sometimes they went down to the river to wash off the dust of the museum with a quick swim. Other times they rode horses now that Noah had gotten a few lessons and Tori was reluctantly getting better at it. Beth's sprained ankle had healed quickly, but the doctor had warned her to take it easy for another week or two.

Noah even found himself considering spending the rest of the summer in Evonia instead of heading home early. Beth and Tori simply assumed he was staying. Beth had already made a list of all the shops and restaurants they would have to try when they had time to visit Alaborn. And Tori was planning a road trip to the south of the country so that they could visit her parents on an archaeological dig. Noah had to admit, he was far more excited for Tori's plans than Beth's. Still, he hadn't told his grandmother or his parents that he planned on extending his stay, partly because he didn't want them to question why he'd changed his mind. He wasn't quite ready to admit the main reason he was tempted to stay: he wanted to spend more time with Tori.

8

The evening before the grand opening of the museum, Noah, Tori, and Beth sat around a table in the library of Rotherham Hall filling out place cards. Noah's grandmother sat nearby working on the seating chart. She had given them each a third of the guest list and instructed them to copy the names out in their best cursive. It wouldn't have been so terrible, except that she made them redo any place cards that were not up to her standards. Noah suspected that his grandmother could have easily had a professional calligrapher complete the cards in half the time, but that she had wanted an excuse to keep an eye on the three of them.

He glanced at the place cards the girls had filled out and felt a twinge of jealousy. His handwriting was standard, neat cursive. It wasn't bad, but Tori and Beth both wrote in an elegant, curling script, complete with artistic flourishes.

Noah's grandmother looked up from her seating chart and watched them without speaking. It made Noah so nervous that he fumbled with his pen, and a blob of ink splatted on the place card. Noah sighed and grabbed a blank place card to start over.

"Why, Annabeth, darling," Noah's grandmother exclaimed, "what lovely handwriting you have! I've always said that good penmanship is a sign of a proper upbringing. What an accomplished young lady you are."

Beth managed an awkward smile. "Thank you, my lady," she mumbled.

Noah's grandmother turned to him. "Well?"

Noah froze. "Well, what?"

"Don't you agree that Annabeth has the most graceful handwriting you've ever seen?"

Beth looked as though she wanted to crawl under the table and hide. "Oh no, it's fine, Noah," she said awkwardly.

Noah cleared his throat to buy himself time before answering.

"Mother," Noah's mom said with a warning tone as she entered the room. "Are you harassing the kids again?"

Noah's grandmother gave her daughter a withering stare, but Noah's mother ignored it. "You sent the butler to tell me that you needed my input on the seating chart," his mom added. "How can I be of service?"

Noah thought his mom looked tired and irritable. He wondered if the transition to being a duchess was more stressful than she let on. *And Grandmother Octavia can't be making it any easier for her*, Noah thought.

"I don't see why we even need a seating chart," his mom continued. "It's a garden party. Most of the time, people will be milling about, eating hors d'oeuvres, and touring the museum."

"Clearly," Noah's grandmother said, "you

don't remember the fiasco that happened at Sir Walter's wedding because they didn't have a seating chart. I refuse to have that sort of commotion at this event. I will not tarnish my dear late husband's good name with vulgar drama."

Noah's mom rubbed her temples. "Are you seriously using *Father* to justify a seating chart? He would have been the one *least* likely to care about who sat next to whom."

"Do you really want to have this conversation right now, Cassandra?" Noah's grandmother asked stiffly.

Noah's mom shot a glance at Noah, as though she had only just realized that he and his friends were in the room. Noah tried to pretend that he couldn't overhear every word of the argument taking place ten feet away. But it secretly made him glad to find out that his grandfather might have shared his opinions when it came to etiquette.

Noah's mom sighed. "Fine, Mother, I will help you with your seating chart. Bring the guest list and come with me to the parlor."

She turned and left, the clacking of her high heels echoing loudly on the marble floors of the hallway.

Noah's grandmother pursed her lips and stared after her daughter for a moment as though she was trying to think of a reason not to follow her. Then she grabbed a copy of the guest list and left the room in a huff.

Tori heaved a sigh of relief once she was gone. Beth relaxed her perfect posture and rested her head on her arms.

"I thought she'd never leave," Tori whispered to the others.

Beth raised her head, her brows knitted together anxiously. "I am so, so sorry about the handwriting thing. I was so embarrassed!"

Noah sighed. "It's not your fault, that's just how my grandmother is."

"But why does she keep singling me out?" Beth continued. "She won't stop trying to throw me at Noah. I didn't complain at first, but now it's just getting awkward . . . I really wish she'd never come up with this stupid matchmaking scheme."

"What do you mean?" Noah asked. He had noticed, of course, that his grandmother had seemed oddly intent on pairing him up with Beth. But he had never figured out why it mattered so much to her.

Beth shook her head in exasperation. "Lady Octavia thought you might not be fully committed to your family's title and Evonia in general. So she invited me to come and spend the summer here, since I was an 'eligible young lady of noble parentage,'" Beth said, making ironic air quotes. "I think she hoped that you would fall madly in love with an Evonian girl and decide to stay here forever." She rolled her eyes.

Noah stared at her in disbelief but didn't say anything. "So when you say 'matchmaking scheme,' you're talking about—like—my grandmother hoping I'd *marry* you?"

Beth flushed. "Not right away, obviously. We're still teenagers! But I do think in her ideal world, we would become a couple and stay together and *eventually* get married."

Noah struggled to process this. "But if she

only wanted me to fall for an Evonian girl, why did she have a problem with me liking Tori?" The question slipped out before he realized what he was saying. He'd just admitted to having a crush on Tori, *in front of* Tori. But this conversation was already embarrassing for everyone anyway—he'd just taken it up one more notch.

"Well . . ." Beth hesitated, then plunged ahead. "Tori's not from a noble family. My, uh, bloodline is a lot more distinguished."

Caring about bloodlines is still a thing? Noah thought. Then he felt ridiculous for being caught by surprise. This was Evonia, after all. Everything was old-school here.

The silence seemed to make Beth uncomfortable, and she continued talking. "And, well, sure, I thought you were cute—I mean, *obviously*, look at you—and I've enjoyed hanging out with you, Noah. But I had to draw the line when your grandmother went from trying to push us together to asking me to keep you *away* from Tori. She even wanted me to be rude to Tori to try to get her to leave Rotherham Hall. Or at the very least to discourage her from hanging out with us." Beth turned to Tori. "But I would never do that to my friends."

Noah could feel his blood pumping. "She really did that? Asked you to try to get Tori out of the picture? She had to invent drama, and—and—*manipulate* everything?"

Beth bit her lip in concern. "I agree, the way she treated Tori is not okay. But I've already told her I don't want to be a part of it anymore, so it's no big deal—"

"But it *is* a big deal," Noah protested. "I never knew I was part of a royal legacy until this year, and now all of a sudden my grandmother expects to set up an arranged marriage for me to—what—maintain the well-bred line of the family? She doesn't get a say in who I do or do not have feelings for! I should have spent the summer doing normal teen things, and instead I'm halfway across the world, sitting in a mansion, wearing an expensive suit, and filling out place cards for her stupid high-society garden party."

Noah paused, and realized how alarmed Beth and Tori looked. He knew he shouldn't have let himself get so worked up. But this new bit of information had just confirmed all of the worst suspicions that had been flitting around in the back of his mind all summer.

He took a deep breath. "I'm going to go take a walk so I can think this through." Noah stood up. "My grandmother can't get away with treating people like this."

9

Noah stormed into the parlor where his grandmother was sitting, with the flustered butler trailing in his wake.

"His Lordship Noah Valmont to see you, Your Grace," the butler announced.

"No," Noah corrected, "it's just me, Noah Fuller—your grandson."

His grandmother looked up from the guest list. "Your mother went off to her room."

"That's fine," Noah said. "I'm here to talk to you."

"What about?" his grandmother asked him impatiently.

"Did you really invite Beth and Tori here just to try to set me up with one of them?"

His grandmother pursed her lips. "No—"

"No more lies, Grandmother, *please*," Noah said. "I know you had some sort of plan—"

"I did, however," his grandmother continued, "invite *Annabeth* here with the intention of setting you up with *her*."

Noah opened his mouth, then closed it again. "Wait, what? That doesn't make any sense. If that's the case then what is Tori doing here?"

"Her presence at Rotherham Hall is an unfortunate coincidence, that's all," his grandmother said with a wave of her hand. "She needed a place to stay while her parents were off on their archaeological dig. I couldn't very well refuse when they had been such good friends of Claude's."

Remembering what Beth had said about bloodlines, Noah said, "Well, you haven't exactly been a welcoming host to Tori. Do you think she's not good enough for me or something?"

"Victoria is a fine and well-mannered young woman from a perfectly respectable Evonian family, but the fact of the matter is that you can do better. You are the heir to the Rotherham title—a member of the royal Valmont family. Lady Annabeth is a much better match."

"Beth is a friend, but I don't like her in the same way that I like Tori. And stop saying 'match.' It's not like I'm going to get married anytime soon. I haven't even graduated from high school yet."

His grandmother sniffed. "We would of course wait until you had come of age, but there's no reason why a formal engagement can't take place sooner . . ."

Noah couldn't believe what he was hearing. "You know what? I'm done."

"Done with what?" his grandmother asked.

"Done with all of this. With your scheming, with the Valmont royal family, with the whole country of Evonia. I'm leaving and going back to America. I don't even want to spend the rest of the summer here, let alone commit to spending the rest of my life here as the heir to the Rotherham title. I'm catching the first plane out of here."

10

Booking international travel was more expensive than Noah had realized. But after he told his parents a short version of what had happened with Lady Octavia, they signed off on Noah's travel plans. The earliest flight to the states was the following evening. As soon as Noah got the booking confirmation, he started packing.

The next morning Noah stayed mostly in his room hoping to avoid any more awkwardness with the girls or tension with his grandmother. He was on his bed, scrolling through his news feed on his phone when he heard a knock on the door.

"Come in," he said, hoping it wasn't his grandmother. He had no interest in continuing their argument from the previous day. He breathed a sigh of relief as his mom entered his room and gently shut the door behind her.

"Hey," she said softly. She was already dressed for the party.

"Hey," Noah replied.

"So, I wanted to talk about what happened between you and your grandmother. Noah, I'm sorry."

Noah looked up at her in surprise. "Sorry for what?"

"For not stepping in sooner." She walked over to where he was sitting on his bed and perched next to him. "I was trying to cut your grandmother some slack. Your grandfather's death hit her so hard. But I didn't realize the lengths she would go to, to keep you here. I never dreamed that she would be so manipulative to her own grandson."

Noah looked up at his mom. "Thanks," he mumbled awkwardly.

"But," his mom took a deep breath as though she was forcing herself to say something she knew he wasn't going to like,

"I think you should stay for the party."

Noah gaped at her.

"—Not for your grandmother's sake," she added quickly, "but for yours. You've spent so much time working on that museum this summer. I think you deserve to see all that hard work pay off." She offered him a weak smile.

"Fine." Noah sighed. "But I'm still leaving right after. I already asked the butler to have a car drive me to the airport this afternoon . . ."

"Fair enough," his mom responded. "You should probably get ready, then. The party is about to start." And with that she left him alone again.

Reluctantly, Noah got dressed and made his way down to the garden. Large canopy tents had been set up on the lawn near the museum to cover the long tables where the meal would be served. Guests arrived in chauffeured cars and were formerly announced by his grandmother's butler. Noah soon lost track of all the people coming in. Other than the occasional distant Valmont relative, he didn't recognize any of the names anyway.

So there he was, milling around with the Evonian nobility and trying his best to avoid his grandmother.

Beth found him by the drinks table talking to the waiter. "Noah! I'm glad you're still here. I was afraid you'd left already."

"Nah," Noah said. "My plane doesn't leave until this evening." The waiter handed him two glasses of lemonade.

Beth looked at the drinks and arched one eyebrow knowingly. "If you're looking for Tori, I think I saw her go into the hedge maze."

"Thank you, Beth—for everything," Noah said.

Beth blushed. "Of course, what are friends for?"

Noah smiled appreciatively.

"Oh, and just so you know," Beth said, "not all members of the Evonian nobility have the same old-fashioned notions as your grandmother. Sure, some of us are very snooty, but some are the nicest people you'll ever meet. My parents and I live in an apartment in Alaborn, not some giant mansion like Rotherham Hall. I mean, yes, it is a very nice apartment, but we don't have servants, or butlers, or five-course luncheons daily."

Another noble called her name, and Beth flashed Noah a quick smile before hurrying off. "Just something for you to think about. Take care!"

"You too!" Noah called after her. Then he headed to the hedge maze to find Tori.

He had already explored the maze earlier that month. The walls were tall and dense, bathing the pathway in cool shadows and blocking out much of the noise beyond. But it wasn't particularly difficult to figure out—it was meant to be a quiet and private place to walk, not as a brainteaser.

Noah found Tori at the center of the maze, sitting on a stone bench near a fountain. She smiled when she saw him, but her eyes looked slightly puffy, as though she'd been crying recently.

"Are you really going back to America?" she asked him.

Noah sat down heavily on the bench next to her and handed her one of the lemonades. "My flight leaves this evening. But I wouldn't have left without saying goodbye." He hoped that didn't sound too dramatic or sappy.

Tori sipped her drink in silence for a moment. "Did you mean all those things you said to Lady Octavia about Evonia?"

"How did you—?"

"Beth and I followed you so we could eavesdrop on your conversation," she mumbled, then shot him a look that was somewhere between a guilty grimace and a mischievous grin.

Noah chuckled weakly. "I don't know, honestly. I'm so fed up with my grandmother and the types of games she's playing for the sake of tradition . . . but I really think I might be falling in love—" he glanced at Tori, who was staring at him, eyes sparkling, and he cleared his throat nervously—"in love with, er, Evonia."

The corner of Tori's mouth twitched into a smile. "With *Evonia*?" she echoed.

"Uh, yeah, you know, its culture, its cuisine . . . its people . . ."

They leaned toward each other and kissed, and for a moment Noah was aware of nothing but being there with her.

Tori's phone buzzed. They broke apart and Tori reached into her purse.

"It's Beth," she said. "Apparently Lady Octavia wants your mom to make a formal welcome speech before we sit down to eat. She's gathering everybody now."

Her phone buzzed again. Tori snorted. "Beth also wants to know if we should mix up all of the place cards on the tables while everyone's distracted."

"I'm honestly kind of tempted," Noah said, snorting back at her.

11

By the time Noah and Tori slipped out of the hedge maze, a crowd had gathered in front of a podium set up on the steps of the museum. Noah's dad stood off to the side as his mom prepared to make her speech. Noah and Tori joined the back of the crowd as quietly as they could.

"Welcome, everyone. First, I would like to thank all of you for the warm welcome my family and I have received on our return to Evonia, as well as your support and guidance as I try to fill the hole left by the tragically unexpected death of my father, Lord Claude Valmont. I hope to be worthy of his title."

"A toast to Lady Cassandra Valmont,

Duchess of Rotherham!" someone in the crowd called. The assembled nobles raised their glasses.

Noah's mom smiled warmly. "But this garden party isn't about me. It's about the grand opening of the Rotherham Museum of Ancient Evonian Artifacts. It was my father's dream that his private collection of Evonian artifacts would one day be open to all Evonian citizens. Because of that, I'm pleased to announce that the museum will have free admission for all visitors. Any charitable donations you choose to make today, as well as any time you visit the museum, will go toward funding children's history programs in Evonian public schools."

There was scattered applause and a general murmur of approval from the audience.

"None of this would have been possible without the help of three amazing teens who donated most of their summer vacation to get the museum ready for the opening. Lady Annabeth Sharpe, Tori Fontaine, and my son, Noah Fuller-Valmont."

Noah smiled. He liked the way his mom had managed to combine the last name he had inherited with the last name he had grown up with.

"Noah, would you like to say a few words to share your unique perspective on this project?"

Noah's smile faded, and the gratitude he had felt a moment before was replaced by a sense of panic. No one had warned him about this. Eyes wide, he shook his head at his mom, mouthing the word "no," but she either didn't see him or pretended not to.

The crowd began to applaud, and Tori gave his hand a squeeze. "Go ahead," she said. "You'll be great."

Encouraged by Tori's smile, Noah staggered up to the podium in a daze. He had never thought of himself as being prone to stage fright. But there was a big difference between presenting a report in front of a class of high schoolers and making up a speech on the spot, in front of the type of people who attended high-society garden parties.

He cleared his throat nervously before stepping up to the microphone.

"It may be hard to believe," he started, "but just six weeks ago, I barely knew anything about Evonia, let alone about ancient Evonian civilizations. I talked with my grandparents on the phone, but I realize now that we missed a lot of chances to talk about the things that really mattered. I wish I could've gotten to know my grandfather better before his death. But I found out this summer that working closely with his collection has been the next best thing. You can really get a feel for someone by looking at what they're passionate about. My grandfather's passion ended up being the same as my passion—archaeology. The Rotherham collection is my grandfather's legacy, and his most valuable contribution to this country. By preserving Evonia's past, we're helping to protect Evonia's future."

Noah paused, feeling like he was rambling and wondering if he was expected to make a longer speech. Luckily, someone in the crowd shouted, "To Evonia's past and Evonia's future!" and Noah took the opportunity to give the podium back to his mom.

His mom smiled and whispered, "You were wonderful." She went to the microphone to announce that the luncheon would be served in fifteen minutes, while Noah ducked into the museum.

Noah was grateful to find the building empty. He needed some time alone to think about everything that had happened that day. He wandered into one of the rooms and found himself in front of the display case with the tiny clay horse. Did he really want to go home and abandon his grandfather's legacy? Abandon Tori?

A quiet cough behind him made him jump. He hadn't heard his grandmother come in.

Noah opened his mouth to speak, but his grandmother held up a hand to cut him off.

"Just listen, please. I am aware that one of my faults is my inability to admit when I am wrong. I cannot excuse personal character flaws just because I am royalty. So I have come to apologize."

Noah was shocked, but he didn't dare say anything yet.

"I made some rash decisions when your mother told me that you weren't sure that you wanted to accept your inheritance as the heir to the Rotherham title," his grandmother continued. "When Cassandra met your father, she loved him so much that she was willing to move to America with him, thousands of miles away from her homeland and family. And I loved Claude so much that I didn't want his life's work to be lost . . ." she trailed off as her voice caught in her throat.

Noah's grandmother took a deep breath before continuing. "In any case, I was hoping that if *you* were able to find the same sort of love here in Evonia, it would convince you to stay. I favored Annabeth—or, I guess, Beth— because of her noble family, but I see now that I misjudged the situation. I am clearly still getting to know my own grandson. Victoria is a lovely girl, and there's no excuse for how rude I've been to her. Her parents' friendship meant the world to Claude, and I know he would have been pleased to see you growing close to their daughter. When I heard your speech just now, I realized that you are so much like your grandfather. And I would be honored if you chose to carry on his legacy for the good of Evonia."

Noah couldn't think of how to respond to this sudden outpouring of emotion. "Grandmother, I—"

"What I am trying to say is that I hope you'll forgive me and consider staying in Evonia, at least for the rest of the summer. There's no need to make any concrete plans about your future, but I have enjoyed having you around, and I don't want to lose you again. I know that Tori and Beth would miss you terribly as well . . . wouldn't you, ladies?" his grandmother stared pointedly at the door.

Noah heard a gasp from the hallway, followed by a stifled giggle. Tori poked her head around the corner, smiling sheepishly. Beth flounced into the room, giving Tori no choice but to follow her.

"We really would miss you, Noah," Beth said.

Tori nodded enthusiastically.

Noah's grandmother smiled. "I must go and make sure that my seating chart is being followed, or there shall be chaos at the luncheon." She winked at them and glided out of the room, effortlessly elegant as always.

Tori and Beth looked at him expectantly.

"Well?" Tori asked.

Noah grinned. "I've heard some very convincing arguments, and I'm starting to think that it might be better if I stayed in Evonia for the rest of the summer."

Beth gave a whoop and flung her arms around him. He caught Tori's eye. She smiled, and suddenly all he could think of was their kiss.

Noah held up his hands, laughing, as Beth stepped back. "Now, just for the record, I haven't made any final decision on whether I really want to move here forever or commit to being the future Duke of Rotherham."

"It's your choice," Tori said. "We don't mind either way, as long as we can still be friends."

"Yeah," Beth said, "we don't care if you're plain old Noah Fuller or Lord Noah Fuller-Valmont von Fancypants."

"I'm going to finish up my senior year of high school in America, but after that, I'm not sure. I'm still thinking about my future plans—maybe college."

"You know," Tori said, "Alaborn University has a great archaeology program. My parents sometimes guest-teach classes there."

The thought of studying Evonian archaeology sounded more appealing than any royal title. Noah's head suddenly buzzed with ideas of how he could expand and improve his grandfather's collection.

"Do you think you'll come visit next summer?" Beth asked. "Oh, please say you will!"

Noah laughed. "I don't see why not."

Beth squealed. "Perfect! I'll make a list of all the activities we can do. It will be difficult to fit everything in. We'll have to get a head start this summer. In fact, I already have an idea of what we can do tomorrow," she called over her shoulder as she headed for the door.

Tori rolled her eyes affectionately.

"It sounds like our schedule is already pretty booked," Noah said.

"I think we have time for one more thing," Tori said, and pulled him in for a quick kiss.

Noah grinned. He grabbed Tori's hand as they followed Beth out into the garden.

RAELYN DRAKE loves to visit museums. She also enjoys fancy parties, but uses the wrong fork more often than not. She lives in Minneapolis, Minnesota, with her husband and rescue corgi mix, Sheriff.